You Have the Right to Remain Silent

... Unless You Talk

YOU HAVE THE RIGHT TO REMAIN SILENT

. . . Unless You Talk

Published by

WISDOMGAME®

Written by

Stephen P. Means

Wisdomgame® - Published 2007

Cover by Stephen Means

ISBN 978-0-9792448-3-4

INTRODUCTION

I've read a lot of self help books and normally I don't read introductions, so why am I writing one? Maybe you like to read introductions, I don't know. You're not me, and if I could read your mind I might be in the circus. This world certainly is a circus too, but I'm not a mind reader.

Maybe you want to know what qualifies me to write a book about breaking through to a life of abundance, health, and love. This is a paradoxical question. Being 'qualified' to do something is a gigantic barrier. It's a concrete wall that takes a huge crane and big metal ball just to make a dent. You'll have to spend a lot of money, get a PhD, and work at least five years with a psychoanalyst to get one of those and then you'll also have to buy an operations manual.

Don't worry about being qualified. With the purchase of this book, I automatically have granted you a 'license' to use the information within to do whatever you want with it, except of course, resell it without paying me. If you are reading this in a library or the coffee shop of a book store, good for you. However, as soon as you put the book down you will forget and your 'license' will expire. If you buy this book, you can carry it around. You can tell your friends about it, or act like a smart ass and quote from it. You can put it in your bookcase and show it off, or put it on your coffee table and put a cup of coffee on it. If the weather's cold you can burn it in the fireplace, or you can even resell it at a garage sale ten years from now. If you buy it, it has a thousand and one uses.

Actually, I don't care what you do with it. I'm already financially secure. Money flows easily to me, without much effort, because I support the Universe and the Universe supports me in all that I do. If you scan it by speed reading, if you read it once, if you buy it and take it home, use it and study it . . . (I suggest this) . . . it doesn't really matter. These words are like magic. This book is your doorway to another life.

Why you're reading this introduction, I have no idea. Like I said, I'm not a mind reader, but that does remind me of a Sufi story. The Mulla was waiting at the boarder with his mule. It was hot and a long wait because the inspector was a very thorough man and he had to check everybody. When the Mulla reached the hut and the gate, the inspector took one look at Mulla's clothes and his mule and thought to himself, "He's smuggling something. I will search everything." Well, this went on and on. Year after year the Mulla crossed the boarder with his mules, but the inspector never found anything illegal.

Finally, after the inspector retired, he was in a coffee shop and saw the Mulla. "Okay, I'm retired," he said, "Now, tell me what you were smuggling?" Mulla looked at him. "Why mules, of course."

Why this introduction? 'Cause I'm sneaking ideas by you without you knowing it.

Wild. Crazy. Stupid. Idiotic! Maybe I am. I don't know. Mom always used to call us that. Until I was eight, I didn't know my brothers' real names. Turned out Mom had three kids and none of them were idiots. Wild is a professional speculator. Stupid's worth ten million bucks and sits on his ass all day. I'm not crazy and I'm not an idiot, and I don't have to write books like this for a living. I like to write books.

Well, maybe I am crazy . . . Which reminds me of another story. A young man was looking for the meaning of life. He heard about a guru on top of Pryramid Peak about twelve thousand feet up. Well, it was a long hike, sometimes without a trail and metaphorically speaking, more like a grind. At last, he came to the old one's hut and got on his knees and begged for the answer. The old man said. "Do you know how a dog poops?" The young man looked quizzical. "Not really."

"Do you know how a cow poops?" Was this a trick question? "Not sure," replied the young man.

"Do you know how a horse poops?"

"No," replied the young man.

There was a long pause. The guru jumped up. "You come here and take my time. And. you . . ."

"What?" asked the young man.

"You don't know shit!"

Well, dear reader, you're not the seeker and I'm not the guru. In fact, the opposite is true. You're the guru. I'm nothing and you know everything. I don't know anything and you're the guru because you know a considerable amount about me already. You know I don't read introductions, I don't believe in barriers, and I learned everything I know in the restroom of my forth grade grammar school. That last part's not really true, but I do know a lot of dirty jokes which is somewhat paradoxical, because jokes depend on timing and in this book I absolutely prove, beyond a shadow of a doubt, that time does not exist.

"Beyond a shadow of a doubt." That's a funny statement, if I ever heard one. Think about it. When you cast a shadow, the light of day is beyond it. But what kind of shadow can doubt cast? Doubt's empty. It's a state of mind of not believing, which is one hundred percent sure of not being sure. Maybe when you doubt, you're full of yourself. In that case you'd cast a big shadow on everything. Thinking about it kind of twists your mind up and wraps it around itself.

Next time you're all twisted, lay on your side with your head on your pillow and say "Wish I may, I wish I might, wish upon a star tonight. If I should die before I wake, may God my soul to take." As you lay on your pillow, you will feel a little moisture run out your ear. Oh no. You're loosing your mind. Sometimes you have to loose your mind to save your soul.

Doesn't matter if you speed read this book or **take it home and practice it**. (I recommend this.) You can understand, even as your read these words, the world is changing, and you're changing. My old boss used to say when a pretty girl walked by, and my eyes bulged out of my head and followed her behind barking up her legs and drooling; he'd always remark. "All cats are grey in dark." That's what we're doing right now. We're in the dark embracing the cat of change.

This book's not about change. It's not about how to change. It's

not about anything. It's a blazing hot poker that cauterizes your

festering. It's a vice that compresses your self and produces a self-

healing salve for those wounds. It's radical. It's innovative. It's a

revolution beyond anything you've ever experienced, and such a

sophisticated brand new technological breakthrough that if you can

understand it, send me a note, and let me know what it really is

about. Buy my book, read it once, you're cured! Buy it again, read

it twice, you're unlimited. Buy it three times, read it three times,

you're nuts and I'm rich.

DEPOTENTIATING FRAMEWORKS

The purpose of the following is to remove the barriers you hold in your conscious mind. The writing that follows uses humor to remove the road blocks and tear down the brick walls which keep you from enlightenment. This work is written strictly as entertainment.

Disclaimer

This book is only for entertainment. Contained within the following pages are physical and mental exercises. Always check with your doctor before attempting anything strenuous. While **WISDOMGAME®** provides these exercises solely to **entertain, educate, and enlighten**, in doing these exercises you accept responsibility for any changes which occur.

START HERE

If you are here for the first time, look! You're going to have to start doing things a little differently. Following the rules got you where you are right now. You wouldn't be reading this book if you weren't at least a little curious about creating something new, or having more life, or attracting something more and better. If you started here, go somewhere else and start there. Stop reading this, and if you don't stop and you continue reading this . . . it just proves you always get what you deserve. So thumb through to another part and read that.

You deserve an unlimited life.

Okay, very good. You did well. You're reading this right now. There is no doubt about it and that goes to prove that time does not exist. Again, it's right now, and I want you to remember back to your days in school. If you didn't go to school, that's okay, you'll still recall this because it's in everyone's memory bank. Italian philosopher, Descartes, of the sixteenth century coined the phrase, 'I think therefore I am.' So, 'I think' is equal to 'I am.' This could be expressed as I think = I am, and since both sides of a mathematical equation can be reversed, I am = I think. It is apparent what Descartes was saying is I am I think. I doubt if it was I think I am. That doesn't make much sense.

This may be spurious logic, but at least one thing we do know is that *you think you are*. Right now, I'm not sure what I think. But this book's not about me. You can read the introduction if you want to know about me. This book's about you. The question is not if you think you exist, it's **who do you think you are?** . . . and **how are you going to get what you want?**

So you remember being in school and all that reading that put you to sleep every night, and you have a lot of other memories of this, that, and the other thing, and it all fits in sort of a time line that goes back to pictures of when you were a little baby. I have to be brutally frank with you: **All that's an illusion.**

The concept of time as a line is incorrect. Even if you believe the images in your head are close representations to what happened, in our universe no natural straight lines exist. Universes, solar systems, planets, and atoms follow spiral paths. There is no such thing as a straight line. Even a straight line drawn with a pencil on paper is simply a series of dots and as you get real close it's not straight anymore. It jumps around. So 'straight' doesn't exist. The interpretation of time as a line moving from past to present and future is an idolized extension created by humans to explain and protect us from truth. Which is, we are constantly changing, but time is always eternally now.

You can ask Descartes.

WHO ARE YOU?

And does anybody care about that right now except me and you?
Probably not, or you'd be out cruzin for a bruzin instead of
reading. I care about you because it's my special intent to wake up
a few people, and after reading this book, *stop sleeping*. Hey, wake
up!

**You chose to read this book because you are a special
person. You are unique. The changes you desire are occurring
now. This is the way. You can have as much as you are able to
have. This is the nature of the universe**.

What you consider to be you is an ever changing group of
visual, auditory, and feeling states that come and go and produce
different thoughts and moods. These are retained within and
sometimes, maybe often, cause you problems because something
in those memories is unfinished and incomplete. This is not right
or wrong, good or bad. It's the way we are. When one or two

unfinished color, sound, or feeling states monopolizes our lives, we can get attached to this position and this prevents us from feeling fulfilled.

Time is an illusion, but we're not concerned about time. We're concerned about you, about breaking through the barriers which bind you in any way. What you need to do is complete those unfinished situations. How do you do that? That's a good question. You can't go back in time. Even if you could, it wouldn't be the same. You'd be bigger or older and nothing would be like you remembered it. So what can you do?

You can apologize and forgive people who are still around, and you can also change memories by redoing them and completing them, and in your day to day operations you can complete situations and not leave anything unfinished.

What happens after you do that is sometimes called 'quickening,' 'awakening' or 'enlightenment.' By resolving all unfinished memories and keeping new situations from becoming unresolved, you free the energy necessary for break through.

NOW

The ever present moment of now it the only time we have. This is important to remember, and you won't ever be able remember it. It's a paradox. It's Zen, which reminds me of a story about two monks.

Eraserhead and Zip were young monks at the inner city monastery. The master asked them to drive the van over to the other side of town and pick up a load of rice cakes. Only thing was, outside it was raining cats and dogs. It was a long drive and Eraserhead didn't like taking the freeway because he got flashbacks. So they took a route through town. Zip didn't care, it gave him more time to study, recite, and pray.

Halfway back with the van stuffed full of rice cakes, the rain, sleet, and hail got so heavy you could hear cats barking.

Eraserhead stopped at a light and wiped his hand on the steamed up window.

"Gimme something to wipe off this window."

"Maybe we should call the master."

"Gimme the edge of your robe."

"No!"

"Come on squirt. The master wants these rice cakes."

"Use your own robe!"

"Hey!" Eraserhead pointed, "On the curb," he yelled, "what's that!?"

A shapely young girl with her body showing through her drenched clothes hitchhiked at the light. Eraserhead jumped out of the van, opened the door, and shoved her on top of Zip.

"What!" cried Zip.

"Where you headed?" Eraserhead asked as he got back in.

"Anywhere dry," the young girl replied. "Couple blocks, Sally."

Zip fidgeted and blushed and looked up at the girl in his lap.

"Your name's Sally?"

"No. Jill. I'm headed to the Salvation Army. You know, the Sally. There it is! Here. Let me off here."

After they left her off, Zip looked at his wet rob and steaming crouch where Jill had been sitting. He berated Eraserhead.

"You know we're not supposed to get near women. Look what you made me do. I just can't believe it. I touched a women. I touched a women!"

They drove on through the rain for a few moments. Eraserhead turned to Zip.

"We picked her up and dropped her off back there. You're still carrying her."

BAGGAGE

No one can remember <u>now</u> because the act of remembering is looking back in the past which takes you out of the now, so now is gone on to another time. Bye bye. Nice knowing you, remember me to Harold Square. Tell all the boys down on 32nd street that I will soon be there. Now is sort of a non existent animal. It's here. Then it's gone. You can't put your finger on it before it slithers away and another moment of now takes it's place . . . now, it's gone. Reminds me of a chameleon I had when I was a kid. I'd put him on my shirt and he'd turn the color of my shirt, then one day he bit my finger and wouldn't let go. I finally shook him off, and he disappeared. Now, he's gone, or maybe he's still around and I can't see him.

You can have anything you want.

Everyone is full of it. Baggage, that is. We all carry around emotional states and mental crystallizations which we have built out of unfinished situations so we can prove that we were right and whoever or whatever we can't let go of for whatever reason . . . well, of course, they are wrong. I must be right about this. I thought a lot about it, and I've really invested a lot of time and energy in writing this book. I am right! Actually, it's not really baggage. It's in this leather bag here, but viola! It's not baggage, it's a tool kit.

The first tool is like a screw driver. "I won't like you anymore if you don't agree with me."

The second tool is kind of like wrench. "Been there. Done that. I know. Let me tell you!"

Sometimes, it's a hammer. "You're stupid!"

Sometimes a sledge hammer. "Damn you. You idiot, %@*# you!"

If none of these tools work, finally there is a little jewel box. When you open it, it sings a sad little song and moths flit into the air. They're all those unfinished situations which you use now to make yourself right and keep you in your box.

Look inside: Larva.

The jewel box starts singing a little tune from kinder garden. "The worms crawl in. The worms crawl out. The worms crawl over your greasy snout."

DEATH

I don't want to talk about death. So I won't. I'll just stare in a certain direction and put one finger up to my lips and keep quiet. Don't look over your shoulder right now, because if you do you won't see my chameleon.

When you die, the door of the hold on your jet to Heaven will open and all that baggage you're carrying around will blow out and disappear. But right now, you can't grab hold of the moment because the moment's always gone. So what are you going to do? You see your baggage flying out innuendo, and you can't hold on to the now.

In the last century, Krishnamurti was considered the teacher of the age. When I was young, I listened to him in the Oak Grove in Ojai. He spoke softly. You could hardly hear him, much less figure out what he was talking about. Later, I read everything I could find that he'd written. He's hard to crack, but here's the meat of the nut: Your mind is fear.

Most people are afraid. But I'm not saying he said most people are afraid. That too, but the point is the mind itself is fear. Specifically, the thinking that goes on in your head, the psychological process which define you as you, is the creation of a personal time line so as to defeat the coming extinction of that created time line. In other words your mind exists as a process or means to prove to itself it exists and will exist after you die; in reality, it doesn't exist at all and is simply fear. Your mind is fear.

I don't want you to think about death. You might get scared. Think like this:

Once upon a time, in a womb surrounded by warm nurturing fluid, you lived happily ever after.

Just kidding. If the door is going to open for you, you have to die before you die. The you that is your baggage which is fear has to die if you are really going to be born. To do this you **really don't need to understand why people create tool bags and jewel boxes**. If you want, right now, you can **simply take out the garbage**. In your mind's eye, put all your 'shoulds' and 'oughts' into a plastic bag and **throw them out**. If not, keep dreaming.

I certainly am. I hallucinate that you enjoy using this book. So after I go out and mow the lawn, I am filling up some more pages.

TIME MARCHES ON

Wow. I've got a big lawn, but it's a pleasure to be outside and the mower does most of the work. I just walk around and then dump the bag. I could pay a gardener, but I like doing it. It's good exercise, and it proves a point. Not that I have anything to prove, but it only took a second for you to turn the page or to read this while I was out in the morning sun mowing my lawn for forty minutes. Time is relative. Sometimes it might seem to be speeding along, but most of the time it goes in a spiral.

Your mind doesn't work in a straight time line either. It associates or links memories, feelings, and states of mind to similar and opposite links. It jumps around like a monkey. You can put that monkey on a leash and chain and give him a cup and grind out a sorry tune day after day, but you won't get what you deserve.

You deserve unlimited prosperity.

Or you can understand the monkey and cut it loose. Maybe it'll get a job in New York City in a big corporation and bring home some real money.

The mind jumps around like a monkey because it's afraid to look at its coming extinction. You get caught up in this activity when you harbor unfinished situations. This is why you have to die before you die. You need to finish all the unfinished situations which is the you, you have created. Then, when you actually die, who knows what happens. We're not concerned with that. You need more life now.

No one really knows what happens when we die. That's why there are so many different religions and concepts of the afterlife. You can spend a lot of time dreaming and hallucinating and picturing a heaven, but in this book, we're not concerned about this. Rather . . .

Bite the ass of life and drag it to you.

OPEN THE DOOR

When you begin to see how your thinking works, you open the door to a new reality. The only time there is, is right now, so let's open that door. Go into your thoughts and create a long hallway. It's dark. You can feel your way along the walls and you can kind of tell there is a rug on the floor and up ahead it's getting a little lighter, but it's still too dark to tell what's ahead. It's like you're in a long tunnel but there's enough light to see that it's a hallway, and up ahead you notice, in the ceiling, there's a skylight. It is open and as you look up you see dark clouds that seem to be moving in a blue sky and now the clouds part and a ray of sunlight streams down into your eyes. You can look directly into this sunlight, and the energy of your mind streams into you.

You is bigger than you think.

The memories, pictures, feelings, and associative links in your mind can be changed so they link to pleasure and enjoyable states. Let's go back down that hallway for a moment. Until the light came in the skylight, you didn't notice some framed pictures on the wall. Now, as you notice them, you can see the glass is dirty and the frames are worn. Rub the glass, you see there's a picture of you when you were young and growing up. There's lots of pictures of you and even some pictures of a you as you thought you'd turn out. A couple of them show a big rock candy mountain and a floating pie in the sky. We'll leave those behind for now, and gather up some others and head down to Don's shop.

You are bigger than your pictures of you.

DON'S FRAME SHOP

Don owns a frame shop. He's a nice friendly Jewish chap. One of his heroes is Viktor Frankel. You remember Viktor. During the holocaust, the Nazi's threw him in prison and every day was torture. Viktor survived by positively reframing his thoughts so that he was going to get some good out that horrible experience. And he did, more than he imagined, because you are at Don's shop right now learning how to reframe your experiences, and Don learned a lot from Viktor.

****

Hi Don, how are you?

"Good to see you. How are you?"

Good. This is a friend of mine. (You.) We wanted to find out if you could help us with these pictures.

"No problem. Looks like the glass is okay. Maybe you need new frames."

What do you suggest?

"Well, let me show you my process. You see this picture. It was left here this morning. See, it's a picture of a boy and his mother. The frame is really old and tarnished."

Yeah.

"Well, turn it on. Hit that button. Now, what do you see?"

Looks like mommy is shaking her finger at the boy. What's that she's saying?

"You'll go blind. Hair will grow on your palm. You'll never grow up and if you do you'll be weak. When the time comes you won't have any left. Stop it, or you'll go insane."

"Mitt en der slanger," as Freud would say.

How do you change that?

"Well, in this shop. I don't actually do the work. I just provide the materials and give the advice. My advice to him is first clean the glass and put a nice gold frame around the picture. That makes it very pleasant to look at."

Yes.

"The boy is obviously hen pecked so we change the picture. Mommy becomes a little hen. See, now he's bigger than his mommy who is now a hen. And see how as the hen gets small, maybe even we put a few golden eggs in the picture. . . Turn it on now. . . . See how much more fun it is. The boy's a lot bigger and even has a smile on his face."

"Squack, squack, squack."

"Every time the hen squacks the boy laughs. Whenever he looks back at that picture he'll feel good."

YOUR PICTURES

Everybody is different, then again, we're all similar. We all have situations in our past where were we smaller, weaker, and felt trapped by circumstance. You have three pictures you brought to Don's shop. Clean the glass of the first one. You will notice that this is a limitation you are experiencing right now. It's a condition you want to break through. See if you can see through the glass even if it's darkly, and make out, if you can, what's going on. That shouldn't bee too hard. It's the reason you picked up this book and it's what you are going to understand right now as you clean the glass.

You are more than the sum of your past.

That's good.

Now, there is another large picture which has to have the glass cleaned also, but for right now, set that one aside. Take the smaller picture, the one with the really old frame and clean it with Don's special fairy dust and Freud's slip so you can see what happened to you a long time ago.

Good.

Now, hit the button and look and listen to the little movie that's playing out.

This is something that happened to you a long time ago. You may not want to look, but you can't help yourself. It may not be pretty, but until you look at it **you can't help** but look at it. It's linked to the first picture you cleaned, which is where you are blocked and it is also linked to the second picture which you as yet are not yet able to see into, which is very important, but we save it for later. Yes?

Concentrate on that small picture. Hit the button. Turn on the little movie. What is going on?

Now, make that picture smaller. Make it smaller still until it's the size of a postage stamp. Make it as small as the head of a pin. How do you feel about that picture?

Bring that picture back to its original size. Now, if there is anyone in that picture besides you, change their head to Mickey Mouse. Make them talk like Donald Duck. Make yourself larger in the picture. Or, if you want, erase the picture completely, and put in different characters so it makes you laugh. Change it someway which makes you happy.

Look at the first picture of where you were blocked. Now, has anything changed?

Join the Club

I lived in Santa Barbara for a long time, and one year I noticed a club started up called the "Center of Attention Club." A group of people met once a week and paraded through the streets and the malls. One by one they would exchange places so that on that day each person got to be in the limelight for a little while and experience what it was like to be the center of attention. It reminded me of the time in grammar school when the big boys dragged some poor chap along and threw him into the girls' bathroom. I didn't like that very much, and when I thought about the Center of Attention Club I knew they were bound for failure because the whole idea was redundant.

Everyone craves attention.

. . . and they get it.

Babies want food and we learn immediately if we want food we have to have get Mom's attention. Life passes in the blink of an eye, and shortly getting food is less of a problem than getting attention. You can feed your family, feed your friends, feed your co-workers, feed your nation and the world if you open up your eyes and ears and see and hear the needs of others and give them attention. This opening up is breaking your outer crust. By understanding that everyone, even you, needs to be in the forefront once and awhile. . . . that people **need you** to see them and listen to them . . . you crack your own shell. You *shell out* when you *pay* attention.

Everyone wants to be the center of attention, but because of unfinished situations, those danged pictures again, in which they got thrown into the girls restroom, or tried to dance, or were put down by a parent . . . they may attempt to get attention by overtly shrinking away from attention. Some people are playing 'hide and seek.' They're hiding behind their own façade waiting for you to discover them.

Feed people with your attention. It will make you powerful, and when you need attention, join the club.

Create your own center of attention club.

The Most Unfinished

What's the most unfinished stone in everyone's jewel box? It's the need to be right, is it not? I'm right, aren't I? It *is* the need to be right, right?

Imagine how hard it was to be a communist in the 1950's. It's okay to be a lefty, right?

Dressed in his three belled hat, little pants, and stripped shirt, the jester appeared before the King.

The King adjusted his golden crown and shifted his butt on his thrown.

"I'm bored!" he said. "Make me laugh."

The Jester laughed. "Don't let it get stuck in your craw."

"What?"

"I said, tuck in you're jaw."

What!?"

The Jester shouted. "It's your mother in law. Mother in law!"

The King was hard of hearing. "Oh yes. Ha, ha. My mother in law. Now say something funny or I'll have your head."

The Jester thought for a short moment, and then jumped, clicked his heels and laughed and smiled. "I'm kidding."

"What?"

"I said, I'm kidding."

"What?" cried the King.

"I said," shouted the Jester, "I'm kidding!"

"What?!" shouted the King.

"I'm kidding! I'm kidding. I'm kidding!" wailed the Jester.

"Off with his head," screamed the King. "You can't be King. I'm King!"

The need to be right comes from our parents making us wrong. As kids, we constantly heard "No!" Kids are curious and make a mess with you know what, so everyone heard a lot of "you're wrongs." These are unfinished situations. How do we make them right?

You can't because you weren't wrong. Your parents and teachers weren't wrong either but perpetuated a chain of violence from their parents and teachers which says curiosity is wrong. It's not wrong. Making messes is natural. It's human. Right?

Now, however, you're a grown up. You have to clean up after yourself.

Not really. I'm kidding.

BIG BRAIN

There was a movie when I was young about some scientists who saved someone's brain and kept it alive in a large tank. Then there was an accident and radiation leaked all over the lab and the brain got contaminated and started to grow. It gained power and got the ability to control the scientists, and as it grew it began to take over the world. You have to wonder about the intent of the big brain. Maybe find a pretty girl, give her a brain enlargement, settle down and have little big brains.

Your mind can decrease and increase its size. The period at the end of the last sentence is ink on paper. In your imagination you can shrink yourself down on the paper and see the ink. You can go further and see the molecules of ink sitting on the molecules of paper. You can go on and on, shrinking to the atom, the electron, and the tiny nucleus.

Also, you can expand yourself to float above the blue orb of the Earth, and you can go into outer space to sit on the sun and go more and more and look back at the Universe.

Your center holds power

I don't want you to go so far down or so far away that you seem insignificant. Try this, go to a point exactly in the middle of your body, a few inches above the place where you were connected to your mother. Silly, your belly button . . . That is, see if you can put your awareness as close as possible to your center.

Good. Now, in your mind's eye, look down at your feet as if they were miles and miles away from you. Now, look back at your head as if it were miles and miles away almost touching the sky. You are at the center of your body.

Come back into your normal state of mind and relax. You are a very significant person. Soon, and very soon indeed, you will discover what you need to learn and you will apply that knowledge in significant ways to achieve what you intend to achieve.

You are a very important person.

The Device

Dr. Brad Pitt and Professor Colin Feral were sitting in the lunch room taking a break, eating junk food.

"What's that?" asked Professor Feral.

Pitt holds up a small gizmo with tiny flashing lights and a rotating gear. "I borrowed this for my son's science project. He's making something to slow down photons."

"Slow down photons? He must be a brain."

"Yeah, the apple doesn't fall far from the tree."

"Oh. I heard about your wife and the Pizza man. Doesn't your son have a job delivering pizza?

"Why you!"

Sock! Bam. Biff.

Every day in every way life gets better and better

Later, at the end of the movie, Dr. Pitt is in his office overlooking the time displacement machinery. His son, Pithy, comes in with a pizza and his science project.

"Here's your pizza, Dad, and guess what? I just came from the science fair. I won!

"Not now, son, the experiment's at a critical phase."

Professor Feral runs in. "Pitt! The thing is out of control! We need something to slow down the photon time vortex. It's sucking the life out of the world. Ten seconds to doom's day!"

"Dad?"

"Not now, son. . . . Feral! It's doom's day. What are we going to do?!

"Dad? Dad! My science project . . ."

You need a device to help you carry out your intent. This affirmation is a device:

"Every day in every way life gets better and better."

De Vice

But that affirmation probably is not going to work. Instead, I want you to construct in your imagination a large vice like a plumber has on his truck, but big enough for your head. Now, put your head in there and say "Every day in every way my life gets better and better." Tomorrow, when the doctor calls, "You've got a brain tumor," twist the handle of the vice, say, "Everyday in every way my life gets better and better." The next day you crash your car. "Everyday in every way life gets better and better. Day after tomorrow you lose some cash. Then your spouse comes home, "Honey, me and my aerobic instructor are going on a cruise." You get to turn the vice twice and say, "Every day . . . blah blah blah."

Of course, you never know. Next day the doctor calls, "Looks like the vice killed the tumor." Spouse falls overboard, insurance pays a million bucks. A good looking person returns your cash, you fall in love, buy a new car and elope. Day after day in every way my life gets better and better. Really, you never know, but . . .

Affirmations don't work if what you're affirming isn't possibly true. If you say you're rich when you're poor, your subconscious mind knows you're not rich. It knows that's why you are affirming that you are rich. Your subconscious mind is a thousand times bigger than your conscious mind. It's not stupid either. It's already established filters that screen out those types of suggestions. Otherwise all the programs on TV would be programming you. . . . which they do too, because they are much more sophisticated.

Now, there are also very sophisticated methods to change your conscious mind and ways to have your subconscious mind mysteriously provide for you, and I'm going to show them to you later. All the above said, there is one affirmation which will help you now.

I intend to _____**.**

You can put in your own word or words, but I suggest you write "buy several copies of this book." When you intend to do something, it's very opened ended. It's believable. If you hold to it, and focus on your intent every day, this actually works.

The word intent comes from the Latin word, 'intendre' which means to hold attention inward. Attention is very powerful. What you hold inside your mind and attend to day after day, comes true.

I Chews Nuts

I used to go to a produce market where they sold quantity peanuts in the shells. They had a big scoop, but I like the best quality food, so I picked them one by one. As I picked them one by one with my right hand, I got the idea I could train my left hand to do it at the same time. So now, whenever I pick out peanuts I can do it twice as fast.

Talk about the monkey mind.

Anyway, at first my left hand couldn't do it, but then after a few more attempts we were off and running so fast I got done in half the time. After that, I never had to worry about getting work. The Universe is unlimited. Offers came from everywhere. But I'm already living in a circus, no need to move to the zoo.

You can use nuts, or choose to be nuts if you want, but you probably aren't reading this in the produce section of a market.

Now a days it's pretty hard to find nuts that aren't bagged. So instead of chewing nuts, do the next exercise.

A whole mind focuses intent.

Put your hands in front of you as if you're praying. That is, put your palms together, thumbs and fingers touching. Now, clasp your hands and make kind of a big fist in front of you. Don't strain, but hold tightly. Memorize how this feels.

Good. Now open your hands and again put them in front of you, as if praying with you palms together. This time as you clasp them together, notice there is a different way of doing this. The first time, you probably put your left thumb over your right thumb and interlaced your fingers. Now, put your right thumb over your left thumb and interlace your fingers.

There are two ways to do this exercise. Whichever way you did it the first time, do it differently the next time.

One of these feels natural. One may feel a little awkward. Alternate positions back and forth until the feelings blend and both feel natural.

This is the first of some exercises to unify your brain focus and your mind.

Keep reading. It's good for you.

The Map is not the Territory

You always read this in modern psychology books, but I still
haven't figured out exactly what it means. We're not on a hike.
This book isn't your trail head. We're not on a journey. You can't
hear the clack clack clack of the rail under the train. Western
territory? The Sea of Tranquility? Maui? What territory are they
talking about? And why do I need a map? I've got a GPS.

When I first started hiking, my friend and experienced trail
master Vince, and I, climbed around in the Sierras. A few others
were on the trail, and at about ten thousand feet Vince got
separated. A ten year old kid walked by like he was superman and
my legs were molasses, which they were, but eventually I caught
Vince. He was halfway up a snow covered slope.

"This is the way," he yelled. "Just follow my footsteps."

I did. About thirty yards up the snow covered slope, I took another step and fell in up to my waist. This happened several more times until I reached Vince where I noticed other climbers were on a trail, but we weren't. We kicked in shoe holds and forged through the ice and snow and eventually got where we were going, which was more and more adventure.

Life is an adventure

"The map is not the territory" has a lot of meanings. One meaning is what we think we are, is not exactly what we are. Our self-talk descriptions of how we are, is not exactly how we are. What we think about how we think isn't exactly how we think. Our minds are different from the techniques and pathways which we navigate within our minds.

Don't use this book as a map to your mind. It's not. You're

mind is virgin territory. There is no trail head. This is no map.

Moment to moment you are forging your way. You're on the

adventure of your lifetime.

Where's that global positioning satellite when you need it?

Under Arrest

For a long time I studied Gurdjieff, Ouespenski, and Nichole, a study called the Fourth Way. I took it to heart. A process they promote is reading a book three times. On the second read you notice you missed a lot on the first one. On the third read, you comprehend what the author is talking about. You will want to read my book at least three times. I did. It's a classic. I have interspersed tricky phrases and techniques and made them so complicated that you will want to keep at least three other copies in sacred places and always have one ready so you can begin to read it again and again just to understand how simple, direct, and mind changing it really is.

Anyhow, the Fourth Way is about remembering your self. It's a big de vice you put your head into a twist every time you're awake but have allowed the world to hypnotize you into believing you're awake when really you're hypnotized. Here's how you remember yourself. Remember when you woke up this morning. No, that's not it. Remember when you ate breakfast. That's not it. Remember, your last good sex. That's certainly not it. Remember that time as a child when you noticed everything was new. Well, that's closer, but that's not it. You can't remember yourself.

You have the right to remain silent

Or can you? Waking up is a process that you do on your own. Books, gurus and masters can point the way, but their map's not the territory. I'll tell you this. You can compare yourself to the great herd that is the world, and you'll immediately forget yourself and react to day to day incidents as you always do. Moo, moo. Or, maybe you are starting to wake up. Self remembering is looking out at the world and at the same time looking at how you respond to what is happening right now. You begin to wake up when you see you are a reactive, mechanical person. Waking up continues when you notice a small opening in your reactive self, and you stop reactions. You arrest reaction.

You have the right to remain silent.

Why Try?

Why try? That sounds awfully negative. I wonder what Nappy Hill, and Vincent Orange Peel would think of that. It doesn't sound like positive thinking, but it is. Content depends on the context. Let me rephrase that if I have enough time. One last *try* . . . **"Why try . . . when you could succeed."** Yes! The buzzer rings. The ball goes through the hoop from outside the line. Three points! At the last instant, success!

Context and content are different. Context is the relationship to place. Content is what's inside the place.

I have a woman friend who is listening to a tape series called subliminal winning. I told her be careful with that series. You don't know what they're saying. All you can hear is music or ocean waves. Maybe the actual name of the series is subliminal wiener and later you'll go the doctor and get an add-a-dick-to-me. The context of the subliminal is listening to pleasant music. The content is repeated affirmations. I thought the joke was funny, but she didn't laugh. I guess she took it out of context.

Success is defined only by you.

Why _not_ try?

You can figure this out right now. Here's an exercise: Put this book down for a second. Now, try to pick it up. Reach over and _try_ to pick it up.

Good.

Now, did you pick it up? If you picked it up, you didn't _try_ to pick it up. You actually picked it up.

Trying is reaching out to do something, stopping, reaching out, and stopping.

Success is doing.

You can be successful in any place at anything. The context and content of success is only defined by you. You're the master of your destiny, are you not?

Let me ask you. Did you do the exercise above? Did you try it?

The Master

Another important idea from the Fourth Way is stressed while you have your head in the vice of self remembering. They point out that inside your mind there are a lot of different people who alternate taking control of your ship and steering this way and that over your ocean of life. You get up in the morning and continue your day hypnotized by the illusionary time line life you're leading. This is your context. The content of your mind moves from one "I" to the next "I" to the next who designate themselves as the same consistent master as every other "I." Maybe occasionally they are the same and maybe not, but what matters is there is never a permanent captain and so your ship sails on and on toward perfect storms that somehow keep repeating themselves.

Your personality is not your essence.

These Fourth Wayfarers also teach that there is something within every person that is consistent, deeper and true. . . your essence. While different personality 'I's' guide you day to day in different ways, your essence is really who you are. It is as if you are a peach and the seed within is your essence.

When you are able to see that you are a reactive, mechanical person and you stop, then you begin to die before you die. The "you" that dies is the constantly changing montage of false captains who have been steering you this way and that. As these false identities become exposed, they provide fertile ground for the seed, your essence, the seed that is really you, to grow.

Soon, in your day to day life, awaken feeling alive, refreshed, viewing a new world.

You must die before you die.

Hypnotism

You may or may not have realized it yet, but you're being hypnotized. Deeper. That's right. Feeling good. You are a positive person. Now, and from now on, you awaken to a life full of prosperity and health. The Universe supports you, and because you support the Universe, money and love and happiness flows to you. You are a magnet for the things you desire. Deeper. That's right. At this level of mind all the good, all the life, all the abundance which is your birthright flows to you. That's good, very good indeed. It sure sounds good.

You are in a trance, are you not?

Once, a mother duck sat on a clack of eggs, one of which was very large. One by one the eggs hatched and fine little ducks emerged. But the big egg took longer and the mother duck was concerned. What if something was wrong? And when the little duck broke out of its shell, it looked like something only a mother could love. It was big and gangly and waddled around with two left feet. All the other little birds made fun of it and then left it alone.

It grew up depressed. Then one day a large white bird landed in the lake, and how the little duck wished it were so beautiful. It climbed on a rock to see the new bird which was a swan. When the little duck looked back at itself in the water, it saw its reflection. It too was a swan!

Your essence is beautiful.

This is an old story. It is a metaphorical representation of how we allow the world to hypnotize us into thinking we are what it tells us we are. Emerge from your egg. You have been hypnotized. Wake up.

You are a beautiful creature.

TV or not To Be

I'm so old I remember when we got our first TV. Most people don't. For everyone, at least in the rich world, TV has been around all their lives. When I was about eight, I almost chopped off the little toe on my left foot and after Dad took me home from the hospital we stopped and bought a new black and white.

TV will be around forever until something like holography replaces it.

Now, people can see themselves in the womb and see themselves dying on the monitor. My friend, Vince the trail master, says if he knows he's about to die he's going to head to the wilderness and hike until the end. TV lasts a lifetime and in between, it serves as baby sitter, housemate, therapist, and giant eye that hypnotizes you to buy and buy more.

But you know all that.

TV hypnotizes because it works exactly like the mind which is based on good, better, and best. How we think, is a comparative process. I like chocolate ice cream as **good** as vanilla but I'd *better* not eat a lot of it, if I want to feel my *best.* Advertisements come into your brain and tell you that you can have a better life, possibly even the best life. This means your life now is not as good as it could be. Even if you have last year's model, you could have a better model, or the best model. If you don't take the best drug, you're going to have a heart attack. You're going to have a heart attack?! . . . And guess what, you get so mad at the TV . . . you have a heart attack. But you know all that.

Turn it off.

What you don't know is that the rhythm of advertisements is syncopated to your brain waves and the impressions are designed to fill but not satisfy. This is the state of someone who only eats fast food. They are full with little nutrition so they come back and buy more because they're always hungry. When you buy the product advertised on TV you satisfy the craving, but that only lasts for a short time, then you're hungry again. But you know all that.

What you don't know probably won't kill you, but it might drive you insane. It probably already has. It did me. I'm the first to admit it. There's only one cure. Turn it off. But you already knew that, but you can't, because you're hypnotized.

Turn it off.

Three Foods

For excellent nutrition a person needs to eat a varied diet. You can exist on junk food but you're going to get fat and have a nasty case of diabetes. Also, the human animal needs more than food and water. You can survive for maybe a few weeks or more without any physical food, and you can live for about four days without water before you die from dehydration. You also need clean air. Later on I'm going to show you an interesting exercise that greatly increases your mental ability, but right now I want you to think. What else do we need besides food and water?

Think tank depravation experiments have proven that humans go straight to the loony bin without some impressions entering their senses. So let's call a carrot a carbohydrate, air oxygen, and sense impressions, what you taste, touch, hear, and see . . . we'll say all of them are food. What kind of food are you eating? If you're eating carrots from the bin behind the market, breathing polluted air, and only watching TV you're a lot like me and everybody else. The point of all this is:

The quality of your food determines the quality of your life

There are millions of books about nutritious diets and clean water. There are several good books about breathing methods and quality air, but there are few books about taking in sense impressions which feed you and provide your mind with nutrients. For instance, visualize the following. "Goop," "Slime," "Blood," "A large red rose," "An orange sunset," "A child's smiling face." Most likely the latter images make you feel better than the first ones. They feed your mind.

This is another reason TV is not so good for you. It feeds your mind images of death, destruction, heartache, and violence.

A movie producer was heard to remark, "We don't force people to go to movies. Sure we show movies with hypnotic color images larger than life but it is art, and the viewer suspends disbelief.

There is no relationship between going to movies or watching them

on TV and violence in our society."

Really? I didn't know that.

I thought you were what you ate.

But you knew that.

Out of Mind; Out of Sight!

The rule when you park your car anywhere is 'Out of sight, out of mind.' It's obvious that thieves won't steal something unless they know it's there. Hide your goodies and you get to keep them. The converse is also true when dealing with the junk in your mind. I'm not just 'trying' to be funny. When you get a load off your mind, it is out of sight! The problem is, much of the stuff we'd like get rid of we hid so no one would see it, and now we can't find it either.

I want you to get a journal, or a couple of pieces of paper you can throw away, because you'll never read them again anyway. When you've got something to write with and write on, then write: "I remember when . . ." You fill in the rest. I'll help you get started. "I remember when a bee stung me. Or, I remember when I rode a pony. I remember when I met my very first love. I

remember when Mom or Dad . . . or, I remember the first time that
I . . ."

Once you get started, you'll find it hard to stop. Stuff will come
flowing out of you almost in an endless stream. If you ever went to
school, you have a lot of practice doing this. You studied, you
studied, and you studied some more, cramming those facts and
figures into your brain. At the end of the week or the end of the
class you puked, that is, disgorged them at the examination. So this
should be pretty easy for an experienced person like you. Unlike
taking an examination, writing your experiences is fun. No one's
judging you because no one's going to look at them again, even
you.

It's true. In 1978, Perk and Winkle did a study of one thousand
college students. For one year, each student wrote in their journal
every night. In 1998, twenty years later, researchers contacted the
students. Amazingly, none of the thousand college students could
even remember being in college.

Journaling is cathartic. That's the purpose.

Heal Yourself

Here's the root of the problem. If you get so ill you need to go into the hospital, you may not come out. Statistics show that a major cause of death are mistakes made in hospitals due to incompetence, neglect, and understaffing. You don't want to go to a hospital if you can avoid it. Another problem is that the cure for your disease may actually kill you. "We got rid of the disease, but the patient died." The idea behind chemotherapy is to take your body to the edge of death and kill the cancer or the tumor and then bring you back to life. The recovery rate for children under two who have chemotherapy is very low. In fact, it's zero.

You have to do what you have to do to cure yourself. You need to be a detective before you accept what the medical establishment tells you. This doesn't mean you shouldn't take the medicine that has been prescribed. However, make sure you do your homework.

Go to another couple of doctors and see if they find the same malady. Search the internet for others who have similar symptoms. Get all the help you can anywhere you can.

If you're ill, see your doctor. Also consider alternative therapies which are holistic in that they not only treat your body but also your mind, and spirit, and your environment. The old saying "garbage in, garbage out" applies to what you put in your system. The 'you' that you are 'now' is a composite of all you have taken into yourself over the years. Spontaneous remission of disease is not the norm. However, it is possible to quickly rebuild.

Doctors are human beings who have lives and families and are sometimes healthy and sometimes ill. They are not superhuman, and they often they don't have the time to spend more than a few minutes with you. You need to come prepared. Have a list with you of the problems you've been experiencing. If your doctor knows you well, this may also be a problem. The doctor may not see your disease as new. Rather, instead of investigating the causes of the disease they may fit you into the mold of your previous complaints. That is, they may tie you to your history instead of looking freshly at your problem.

Your list should include how you have been sleeping, what's going on in your life. If you're having relationship problems, what's bothering you psychologically, are you worried? Tense? Don't allow your doctor to simply prescribe for the symptom you are having. Ask them if they have any clue as to what could be causing your disorder.

Doctors are trained in allopathic medicine. Allopathic medicine is a system that aims to produce a condition opposite or antagonistic to that affecting the patient. The nature of this training focuses on conditions which are symptom specific and tends to exclude the holistic involvement of the patient. Western doctors generally rely on antibiotics which quickly and efficiently cure. However, quite a few are not trained in nutrition or environmental analysis.

Remember that your doctor is a person who comes to work, works hard, is usually overloaded, and isn't perfect. He or she works in an establishment that wants you to have the best care possible. However time is money and establishments need to make money. When you're sick you may not have an abundance of either. What's really important is curing your disease. It's up to you. Find the right doctor, in or out of an established system. Get the best medicine.

You matter!

Take care of yourself!

Laughter is the Best Medicine

It's hard to pin point exactly what the Sufi's are. They're not
exactly a religious cult and they're not exactly a secret
organization. Idres Shaw wrote a lot about them. They won't invite
you to join unless you're serious, which I find strange, because one
of their main teaching devices is humor. Their literature is full of
it.

Laughter, that is.

At the very moment and during expelling a spontaneous guffaw,
where are those problems you thought were so serious? They're
gone. Check it out:

A horse walks into the bar.

Bartender pours a drink and asks, "Why the long face?"

******

Horse's eye twitches and he downs the drink. "I just heard a
strange story. You got time?"

"Shoot. I mean, let me spur you on."

"You're funny. I'm very serial. Let me tell you . . ."

"Go ahead."

The horse whinnies:

"One time, back a few years ago around 1860, an Arabian, let's call him Mulla thought he'd go to school in the US. He moved to New York City and studied law. When he got out of school, he didn't like New York City too much so he thought he'd move out west. He came to town and found a lot of lawlessness and criminals and such, but he couldn't find any work because there weren't much of a legal system then."

"Just like now," the bartender interrupted.

"Just like now," continued the horse. "Anyway, once Mulla got to town he couldn't find a job in law and had to go to work as a bartender."

"Hmm," the bartender looked out the corner of his eye.

"That's right. He got a job in a bar and started pouring drinks for everyone. He really enjoyed himself. Then one day, a large man came in off the street with a wild look."

"Give me a drink!"

Little Mulla poured the big man a stiff whiskey.

"Big John's commin," he mumbled.

Mulla leaned forward. "What?"

"Big John's commin," the man muttered.

Mulla couldn't' quite hear. "Did you say Big John's coming!"

The gambler stopped dealing. "Big John's coming?"

The young dancer put a twenty dollar bill in her stalking garter. Her eyes flashed. "Big John's coming?"

A glass of beer dropped and broke. "Big John's coming?!"

Everyone in the bar went quiet and stopped what they were doing. It only took a moment, but then they were gone. Mulla followed them into the street. Down the street there came a cloud of dust. A giant man with a bright red beard and bright red hair was riding a buffalo, holding onto its horns and jamming his spurs into the buffalo's hide. Mulla ran back into the bar.

The buffalo slid to a stop and the dust welled up. The giant man smashed through the bar door and strode up to the bar. He picked up Mulla and held him to his face.

"Give me a whiskey, now!"

Mulla started to pour a shot.

The red haired monster grabbed the bottle, broke the neck on the bar and drank the whole bottle.

"Thanks! I needed that!" bellowed the big man.

Mulla whispered. "You're welcome, Big John."

The huge red haired man leaned forward. "Big John? Did you say Big John? His eyes rolled in his head. "Big John's coming?" He turned and ran out the door screaming, "Big John's coming! Big John's coming!"

Metaphorical Language

Jokes, myth, legend, and stories are written and spoken with words which talk to unconscious parts of our minds.

Talk to the window to open the door

I used tell stories, and the following is one I really liked to tell. See if it touches something in you. I'm condensing from memory 'The Prince's Visit' by Horace Scudder. I changed it a little.

It was a beautiful day, and there was an expectation in the air you could just feel. The town was full of excitement. The Prince was due any moment. People were walking toward the main street. There were yellow, and green, and red banners everywhere. A juggler tossed balls, and drummers were beating drums. A young boy pushed a hoop along, and the horse parade was ready to start.

This was the day Peter had been expecting all year. As he ran to the backyard of the house, he could hardly stand the excitement.

"Mother . . . Mother, the Prince is coming!"

She took down the last of the wash. "As soon as you do your chores. You have to sweep the floor."

Peter couldn't contain himself, but he did all he was supposed to do and even picked a rose and brought it to his mother. "May I go, now? The Prince's is coming. I so want to see him."

"Alright, but be careful."

As Peter ran toward the center of town where he could view the Prince, he noticed the wonderment of the day. Dogs barked. He could smell the aroma of cooking meats and everyone was dressed in the brightest colors. Men and women from farms and townspeople crowded the streets but Peter pushed on, stepping here and there sometimes even being pushed along with the crowd.

Suddenly, he stepped on something soft.

"Oh!"

Peter looked down. "Who's that?"

A poor hungry little boy, wasted and skinny to the bone, looked up at Peter. "Help me, please, I'm hungry."

Peter looked up at the big people next to him. "Can you help us?"

But his voice was lost in the clamor. Everyone had to see the Prince who was almost to the square.

Without another word, Peter picked up the tiny boy in his arms. "We have food at my house."

Along the street and toward his house, Peter carried the boy while drums beat and crowd screamed. The great celebration had begun.

As he looked down at the poor soul in his arms, the little boy gave a sigh and a little breath, and from the sky Peter heard trumpets. There above the chimneys and the roofs, he saw a host of angles, a chariot and horses, and in the chariot the Prince of Peace carrying the little boy to heaven.

So that day, Peter saw the Prince pass.

Getting Unstuck

Life needs balance.

The first step to establishing homeostasis, that is, balance in your life is to understand the concept that balance depends on motion. Everyone who has learned to ride a bike or to roller skate knows that you can't balance until you get moving. Surfing is the same way. Until the wave begins to surge, the surfer can't stand up. If you're in a stuck in your life, you need to find a way to get unstuck.

How do you get unstuck? The answer seems paradoxical, but it's not. You have to stop doing what you're doing. You need to take some time to yourself and contemplate your life. Whatever your life situation, if you feel frozen or trapped or not in control and unhappy, then you need to look at the situation and simply observe it. Observing your life from this contemplative state is the beginning of the movement of momentum to attain balance.

What do you do when you've dug yourself in a hole? You stop digging.

While you are looking at your life you need to consider if something you are doing to yourself is the cause of your dis ease. Is there something in your diet that you are particularly hooked on? Often, the substances we are allergic to are the ones we become addicted to. And like substances, we can also be allergic to negative people, to animals, and to the place we live, and even what we do for a living. The allergic trapped situation makes a person feel like "I have to have it, but I can't," or "I must have it, but I don't want it."

No one is to blame. When you blame someone else or external circumstances you give them control over you. You're not to blame either, it happened. You make yourself whole by accepting yourself.

You are not to blame.

CREATE YOUR LIFE

Some years ago Maxwell Maltz penned a book called 'Psycho-cybernetics.' That book is _____. (put in your own word: fantastic, revolutionary, fun, idiotic.) Maltz was plastic surgeon and he discovered that it took three weeks for his patients to actually believe they looked better after surgery. His theory is that the subconscious mind is a servo mechanism like a heat seeking torpedo. If you want to program your mind, it takes about three weeks of believing before anything happens. The extended idea is that if you believe you're wealthy and healthy your mind will create that for you.

You can create the life you want

This works. The problem is that not everybody thinks the same. Some people actually think in feelings, some think with words inside their heads, others see pictures.

You can use pictures to unify your mind. If you think in feelings or talk to yourself, you can also participate. All you have to do is pretend you're in a darkened theater and a movie is playing on the screen.

The movie's a little dull, just a picture of some mountains. It's morning and the sun's coming up behind a mountain so the sky on your left is getting brighter. There's a tree in front of you and you can sit down there and watch the sun rise on your left. Now, you notice that the sky is also getting brighter behind the mountains on the right.

You are sitting on the cool ground, resting your back on the tree and you can hear birds chirp as the sky brightens. At exactly the same time, a sun rises over the mountains on your left and also a sun rises over the mountains on your right.

Now, both suns merge to a singular yellow orb rising over the mountains in front of you. As they merge the area you're sitting in becomes three dimensional.

This is the second exercise to unify your mind.

Color Meditation

I used to be in a discussion group. Well, to tell you the truth, it wasn't official. Me and my buddies would meet around five in the afternoon at Nordstrom's café for a cup of coffee. We were inflammatory, expository and often didactic, not to mention that a lot of babes worked there. Often, after getting wound up on coffee and winding down with my friends, I would cross the street and take the elevator to the top of the parking garage and watch the sunset.

Before sunset the clouds darken.

You are standing at a railing. Below you, city dwellers rush home to dinner. Above you, puffy white clouds push at each other creating a trail of blue sky that winds out across the ocean toward silhouettes of the Channel Islands. The mountains in front of you turn dark and where they part the sun is a great orb of yellow fire that seems to be floating on the horizon at the edge of the ocean. It so bright, you look away and now, above you, the white clouds are turning grey and getting dark.

The mountains behind you turn crimson, and you see in the reflection of a far away glass window, the last sparkling orange flame of the sun. The mountains darken. The clouds are grey. The sun is setting. Long trails of yellow dance with red. The clouds above you turn bright orange. The whole sky explodes in color.

Dark clouds explode with color.

Y.H.V.H.

In Hebrew the name of God is Yod He Vau He. You don't want to say that out loud, especially around a Jewish person. You might get crucified. Or, worse, a lightening bolt will come down from the clouds, open up a hole in the earth, and you and the Rabbi next to you will fall together for eternity. Can you imagine?

Naming is categorizing. The alphabet is our way of ordering. It's a means to file information. From A to Z in your hanging file, you have a place for every manila folder. Except that God is bigger than your file system. Where can you put Her? There's no room. We were made in the image of God. God was not made in our image and she doesn't fit in our file cabinet.

I'm a curious sort so I thought I'd find out what those words mean. So I looked them up. In Hebrew, *Yod* is the "creative hand." *He* is the "window looking in." *Vau* is a transitive the verb "opens" or "is tied to." The second *He* changes a bit after the first,

it's "the window looking out." The creative hand opens the
window looking in tied to the window looking out.

**The creative hand opens the window looking in to the window
looking out.**

Something sound familiar about that? Didn't we talk about that
before? Can you remember back to where we talked about self
remembering? It's a big de vice you put your head into a twist
every time you're awake but have allowed the world to hypnotize
you into believing you're awake when really you're hypnotized.
Self remembering is looking out at the world and at the same time
looking in at how you are responding to the world right now.

Don't talk about it. Do it.

Look in to look out.

Know Yourself

Metaphysicians and new age writers are always quoting the words over the entrance to a temple in Delphi as "Know Yourself." I find something very strange about that. Can you imagine walking by and looking at that? What are they advertising? Come in here, study our system, you'll get to know yourself like we want you to. Or, the writers might be misquoting and it actually says "Here's to you. No, yourself!"

Maybe it's deeper than both of those. Maybe it's a symbolic threshold. The saying is on the outside of the building so it must be exoteric. Before you cross to the inside, into the arcane secret world of the inner life inside the temple, into the esoteric, you have to cross the threshold of knowing yourself.

Knowing yourself is not an end. It's a beginning. It's a threshold you have to step over before initiation. . . or, do you?

Now! Enlightenment

Initiation is a scary word. If you look it up you'll find it's defined as a beginning or starting something new and often is connected with secret societies and the occult. There's a problem. Actually, a situation. I don't believe in problems. What initiation really means is the first step in getting your initial, your degree of progression from A to Z so you can put God in your file cabinet. As you move through the process you eventually get to be top dog who not only sits next to Him but is HIM.

Remember what we said before with the name of God, Y.H.V.H; God's bigger than the file system. To begin initiation means to get started on a long road to enlightenment and in this life or the next life, somewhere in the future, you achieve. You become a letter-man, a BMOC on the campus of the spirit. The situation, however, is that **'now' is the only time**. There's no road to enlightenment. It's not gradual. You don't go there through degree. The time's always now. Guess what?' It doesn't take any time. Buddha told me.

Enlightenment

Reality

I was looking for my reading glasses everywhere. First of all, I couldn't see very well but I kept looking. I looked in the office and the bedroom, the kitchen and living room. I looked in the car and outside in yard. No glasses. I couldn't find those danged pair of glasses anywhere. When I finally gave up, there they were on top of my head.

Buddha wrote the Damapada to help me find my glasses. He sat underneath the Bodhi Tree for six years meditating, looking at all the places where I might find my glasses and he came to the conclusion they weren't in his mind.

They were on my head.

He also came to enlightenment when he saw that all the images he had in his head, all the pictures of who he was, were illusions.

It doesn't take six years to find your glasses, but it might take you forever in the search to know yourself. Searching sets you apart from the object of your search. When you are searching, you are attached to what you're looking for . . . which isn't real.

In less than an instant see and drop attachment.

Instantly drop illusions

Again, it's paradoxical. When you realize the truth is you're totally empty, you're totally filled.

THE UNFINISHED YOU

Something has been left unfinished. What is it? If you've been following along, you remember in Don's frame shop there was one picture of you we left for later. The time, as it always is, is now. So clean off the glass and look at the picture. It's you as you really are.

This is your essence. What do you see?

WISDOMGAME®

Wisdom is gained through experience.

Thank you.

You are a beautiful person.